P9-DMQ-991

BOUNCE BACK

ZAYD SALEEM, CHASING THE DREAM

BOOK 3

HENA KHAN

ILLUSTRATED BY
SALLY WERN COMPORT

SALAAM
R E A D S

NEW YORK | LONDON | TORONTO
SYDNEY | NEW DELHI

An imprint of Simon & Schuster Children's Publishing Division
1230 Avenue of the Americas, New York, New York 10020
SALAAM READS and its logo are trademarks of Simon & Schuster, Inc.
For information about special discounts for bulk purchases, please contact Simon & Schuster Special Sales at 1-866-506-1949 or business@simonandschuster.com.
The Simon & Schuster Speakers Bureau can bring authors to your live event. For more information or to book an event, contact the Simon & Schuster Speakers Bureau at 1-866-248-3049 or visit our website at www.simonspeakers.com.
Also available in a Salaam Reads paperback edition
Book design by Dan Potash
The text for this book was set in Iowan Old Style.
The illustrations for this book were rendered in Prismacolor pencil on Denril and digital.
Manufactured in the United States of America
0818 FFG
First Salaam Reads hardcover edition October 2018
10 9 8 7 6 5 4 3 2 1
Library of Congress Cataloging-in-Publication Data
Names: Khan, Hena, author. | Comport, Sally Wern, illustrator.
Title: Bounce back / Hena Khan ; illustrated by Sally Wern Comport.
Description: First edition. | New York : Salaam Reads, [2018] | Series: Zayd Saleem, chasing the dream ; 3 | Summary: When an injury sidelines new captain Zayd, he must find another way to be a leader for his basketball team.
Identifiers: LCCN 2017057095 (print) | LCCN 2018000682 (eBook) | ISBN 9781534412057 (hardcover) | ISBN9781534412040 (paperback) | ISBN 9781534412064 (eBook)
Subjects: | CYAC: Basketball—Fiction. | Pakistani Americans—Fiction. | Family life—Fiction. | Leadership—Fiction. | Middle schools—Fiction. | Schools—Fiction.
Classification: LCC PZ7.K52652 (ebook) | LCC PZ7.K52652 Bo 2018 (print) | DDC [Fic]—dc23 LC record available at https://lccn.loc.gov/2017057095

For Humza
—H. K.

To Ryan and Lizzie
—S. W. C.

ACKNOWLEDGMENTS

As I wrote the third book in this series, I thought a lot about how lucky I am to have such an amazing team around me. I can't thank my editor, Zareen Jaffery; agent, Matthew Elblonk; and members of my writing group—Laura Gehl, Ann McCallum, and Joan Waites— enough for helping me shape this series and bring it to life. I'm also carried by the love of librarians, educators, and fellow writers who make me believe I can do this. Thank you to each and every one of you who has shared my books with a reader, said an encouraging word to me, or made a comment or suggestion that has helped keep me going. A special shout-out to my home team: Edie Ching, Jacqueline Jules, Susan Kusel, Karen Leggett, Kathie Meizner, Kathie Weinberg, and the other wonderful members of the Children's Book Guild of D.C. for being with me over the years and pushing me forward.

Some of the very best things about being an author are getting to talk to incredible kids across the country and globe, receiving letters from them, and hearing that they value what I do. There's no better feeling. Thank you to all of you who I have met, or haven't yet, for reading and making my books part of your lives. I'm grateful to the biggest basketball fans and most valuable players in my life, my sons, Bilal and Humza, who worked with to me to brainstorm ideas, check terms, design plays, and create a winning story line. For this book, I also had my friend Mikail Mirza share his basketball knowledge and creativity when I was struggling to figure it out, along with the enthusiastic support of Zara and Isa

Mirza. My young friend Zayd Salahuddin lent me his first name, along with Musa, Yusuf, Rabiya, Sumaiya, Rania, Suleiman, Adam, and the other special kids in my life who have been so wonderful in sharing their ideas and excitement with me over the years. I remain forever indebted to my parents and family for their endless love, patience, and support. And to my husband, Farrukh—you inspired this series, and continue to inspire me.

1

My new basketball hoop is going to be amazing. I waited forever to finally replace the rusted, bent rim I've been playing on for the past four years. This one has a clear shatterproof backboard like the ones in the NBA. Plus, there's an adjustable height lever you can use with one hand. I chipped in for half of it using the money I had saved up from my birthday and Eid. My parents paid for the rest.

But after three hours and thirty-seven minutes the hoop is still in pieces all over the driveway. My dad is drenched in sweat. My uncle, Jamal Mamoo, is cursing under his breath and probably wishing he hadn't come over today. And I think my mother is pretending to understand Chinese, since that's the only language in the instruction booklet. She keeps rotating the pages to look at the drawings from different angles.

"I think it's the other end that's supposed to go in this thingy," Mama says, pointing at the booklet.

"No. It. Doesn't. Fit. That. Way." Baba has a washer pressed between his lips and speaks through it in a low growl.

"It's too hot outside," Naano declares from the doorway of the garage. My grandmother doesn't believe humans should be in the sun for more than five minutes. "How many hours are you going to do this? Stop now. Come have chai."

I look around in alarm, but no one seems ready to quit yet. My family is the kind that loves to watch do-it-yourself shows together on TV. These are the programs about regular people who tear out their kitchen cabinets or showers and install shiny new ones. We comment on their choices and how all the people seem just like us. Until they start cutting tiles or using power tools. Then we decide they must secretly be professionals.

The do-it-yourselfers on TV are nothing like the Saleem family. We don't usually fix or build anything ourselves. My parents don't own a toolbox or a single leather tool belt. There's only a sagging shelf in the corner of the garage that holds a hammer, a box of nails, random hooks, and a screwdriver or two.

But it cost an extra seventy-nine dollars to get the hoop assembled. So here we are, putting on a bad reality show for our neighbors. I can't prove it, but it sure feels like they are walking their dogs a lot more than usual today and smiling at us extra hard.

"You guys are doing it wrong." My older sister, Zara, saunters outside holding a glass of lemonade and wearing a know-it-all look on her face.

"Zara!" Mama snaps her head up from the drawings. "We don't need your commentary right now."

"Okay. I thought you'd want to know I watched a video with instructions. The guy was NOT doing that."

"Wait." Baba turns around and glares at Mama. "There's a video?"

"There's no video listed on here," Mama says, flipping over the booklet. "Unless the link is written in Chinese?"

"What video?" I ask Zara.

"The one on YouTube. There's a guy who goes through all the steps one at a time for this exact model basketball hoop. You should watch it."

"YOU THINK?" Baba explodes. The lady from two doors down and her tiny yappy dog both jump up, startled as he shouts. I can't help but grin.

Jamal Mamoo catches my eye, drops the pieces of the base he was fumbling to put together, and lets out his wacky laugh. Soon Mama joins in too. Before we know it, we're all howling with laughter. Even Baba. Nana Abu, my grandfather, comes shuffling outside because of all the commotion.

"Hold on a second." Mama puts up a hand, gasping for air. "What's so funny?"

Her question just makes us all laugh harder. I drop to the grass and roll around until my stomach hurts, but in a good way.

Two hours and twenty-three more minutes later, I finally get to try out my Spalding hoop. It's as nice as I thought it would be. Maybe nicer. Best of all, we did it ourselves. Mostly. The dog lady felt sorry for us and brought over her husband and his set of tools to help us. Zara brought out her tablet and kept rewinding the parts of the video until we figured it all out. Nana Abu stepped in for Jamal Mamoo when he left to meet his fiancée, Nadia Auntie, for a wedding-cake tasting. (I volunteered for the tasting job, but my uncle said no way.)

I take a couple of shots and watch them go off the shiny new backboard into the perfectly straight rim. My game is already so much better than it was last year. I'm starting point guard on the team I've worked so hard to be a part of. I'm hoping Coach Wheeler will pick me to be our new team captain now that my best friend Adam left. We've turned our season around and have a chance to make the playoffs. Plus now I can practice at home and not worry about adjusting my shot to make it go in.

"We did it," Baba says. He puts his arm around Mama, and they gaze at the hoop proudly. They're going to have a lot more to be proud of soon. I can only imagine incredible things ahead of me. My future is looking as good as my new hoop.

2

It's extra hot in the gym where we practice. The air conditioner isn't working, and the air feels thick and heavy. Plus Coach Wheeler is running us hard. We did the eleven-man fast-break drill, and I was on defense with Blake. The two of us were trying to stop three people from scoring. I can feel sweat dripping down my back.

"Okay, water break," Coach yells. "Make it quick."

"It's so hot," Blake whines to me. "I'm dying. It's hotter in here than it is outside."

"Yeah," I mumble. It takes too much energy to complain. I glance at the clock. Fifteen more minutes until the end of practice. I'm working up the nerve to talk to Coach about the team captain opening. I'll have to make it quick. It's Thursday, so Naano is going to pick me up since Zara has volleyball, and she hates to wait. Maybe I can get her to take me to Carmen's for some Italian ice. The idea of the delicious fruity ice that tastes like a frozen Jolly Rancher makes me feel cooler already.

"Next up is the warrior drill," Coach says. "Let's give it our all until the end of practice, guys."

The warrior drill is one of my favorites. It's

basically a rebounding-and-put-back battle. A few guys are on the perimeter, and three of us are on the inside. The perimeter players take turns shooting. Those of us on the inside fight one another for the rebound and have to put it back for a score twice before we can get out.

I'm on the inside with Sam and Matthew, and Blake takes a shot from the three-point line. I try to box out Sam. We both jump up.

SWISH!

Blake makes the shot instead of hitting the rim. We turn around and look at him.

"Oops!" He shrugs as if to say he can't help being too good to miss.

"Show off!" Sam mutters.

"Nice shot." Coach nods to Blake. "Come on—let's keep going."

Coach passes Ravindu the ball, and he takes the shot this time and misses. It hits the rim on my side. I've had my legs bent, ready to jump at the perfect moment, and I'm up just as the ball bounces. I grab the ball with both hands and come down hard . . . right onto Matthew's foot.

YOW!

My foot turns in a weird way, and I start to lose my balance. You know how when you start to fall, you actually see yourself moving in slow motion? And there's a moment when you try to stop it from happening? That is exactly what happens to me. Except I can't regain control of my body and put an arm out to break my fall.

THUMP!

I hit the ground hard. The ball pops out and rolls away.

"Hey, man, you okay?" Matthew extends his hand to help me up.

"YEESSHH!" I gasp as a searing pain rips through my ankle.

"Uh-oh. What's the matter?" Matthew looks scared as I grab on to him.

Coach Wheeler comes running over. He puts his arm around my waist.

"Zayd! Be careful. Can you put weight on your foot?"

My heart is racing.

"I don't know," I say.

"It'll be okay. Test it out."

"OW, OW, OW!" I wince as I take a small step, and pain shoots through my ankle up my leg. I have to lift my foot off the floor again.

I feel Coach Wheeler and Matthew look at each other over my head as I stand on my good foot. A lightning bolt of fear runs through me, and I suddenly feel a chill even though I'm drenched in sweat. What did I do to my ankle?

3

The lady sitting behind the counter hands Mama a clipboard and a pen.

"Insurance card and photo ID," she says, not looking up.

"Here you go," Mama says cheerfully. She's always super nice to grumpy people. I think she does it to make them feel bad for not being friendlier.

I'm sitting on a chair in a waiting room at the Rockville Sports Medicine Center, wearing only one of my sneakers. On the other foot I'm wearing a sock. Over that sock, I'm wearing one of Baba's socks, which Mama stuffed with bags of ice.

She had to come pick me up from practice last night instead of Naano. I pretended something was in my eye when I saw her and the tears threatened to flow. Coach helped me into the car, and Zara and Mama both led me into the house. Every time I tried to step on my foot, I had to stifle a yell. I couldn't sleep last night because I kept waking up from the pain whenever I turned over. Mama got me an early appointment with the doctor this morning. So here I am instead of being in school.

"Zayd Saleem," a nurse finally says from a doorway.

"I'll help you," Mama says as I slowly get up. I lean on her and hop over to the nurse, who pats my shoulder.

"Let's see what's going on with you, tough guy. Come this way."

We head into a tiny examining room holding a bed and a couple of chairs. The nurse asks me a bunch of questions, takes my temperature and blood pressure, and clips something onto my finger. It's too much work to get on the scale, and I'm still wearing the homemade ice pack, so we estimate my weight. Finally the doctor comes in, wearing a white coat and big smile.

"I'm Dr. Alam. Nice to meet you," he says, shaking my hand. "What happened?"

"I jumped for a rebound and landed on

my friend's foot and hurt my ankle."

"I see. Basketball player, huh? Rough sport for ankles and knees. Although it keeps me in business." He winks at Mama, and she smiles to appreciate his joke. I don't.

Dr. Alam kneels down and gently unwraps the ice from my foot. He presses in a few spots and rotates my foot slowly.

"OW!"

Frowning, the doctor asks me about my pain level. He points to a chart highlighting a row of cartoon faces. There's a regular yellow smiley face on one end and a bright red crying face on the other. I point to the number seven face: It's pretty upset, but not crying or anything.

"Hmm," Dr. Alam types some notes. "I'm going to need a quick X-ray to check for a fracture."

"FRACTURE?" I sit up straight, and my heart starts to pound faster.

"Don't worry. We'll get you fixed up so you can get back on the court."

The court. My heart still races as I think about how I need to get back to it . . . and quick. There are only a few weeks left in the regular season before playoffs, and I can't afford to be injured. My stomach starts to hurt, so I try to push those thoughts out of my mind and focus on the X-ray machine. It's actually kind of cool to see my leg bones glowing on the screen. They remind me of Jamal Mamoo's nickname for me, Skeletor, which he says is because I'm bony.

When we get back to the exam room, Dr. Alam points to the X-ray images on his computer.

"Good news. There's no fracture."

"Oh thank God," Mama says. She lets out a big sigh, and I see her mouthing a prayer.

Dr. Alam moves toward a drawing of a leg on the wall. "You have what we call a high ankle sprain, Zayd. It's a bit more serious than a regular sprain. That's why you have pain here, in these ligaments."

He says some other things, but I stop listening. My mind is fixated on one thing.

"When can I play basketball again?" I ask.

"I'm hoping in about four weeks, depending on how well you do."

"FOUR WEEKS?" I'm louder than I meant

to be, and Mama shushes me. I keep talking anyway. "We still have games left in our season and need to win to get into the playoffs! I HAVE to play!"

"Sorry, buddy, you need to stay off it as much as possible." Dr. Alam looks at my face and smiles gently. "Tell you what. Come back in two weeks, and we'll reassess."

"Does he need crutches?" Mama asks.

"For the first couple weeks," Dr. Alam says. As they continue to speak, my heart sinks into my stomach. I've always wanted to hop around on crutches. It looks like so much fun. But today, they're the last things in the world I want. All season I've dreamed of taking my team to the playoffs. I don't know how I'm supposed to do that now.

4

Mama dumps a bunch of little bags onto the kitchen table. Everyone is drinking chai and eating Naano's favorite biscuits, which she pronounces "bizcoot."

"What about this one? Isn't it cute?" Mama's holding a small, sparkly gold pouch that has a red drawstring on top. I can imagine a tiny pirate using it to stash even tinier gold coins.

"How about this plain one?" Dad picks up a bag made out of a gauzy white fabric. "It's classic."

We all look at him in surprise, and he shrugs.

"What? I'm trying to participate."

"Nadia and I would prefer to use something recycled," Jamal Mamoo says, which causes Naano to snort.

"You want to give people trash? How about empty chips packets?" she says.

"No, Ammi," Jamal Mamoo explains. "We're thinking of little Chinese-take-out-style boxes made out of recycled paper. Nadia found them online."

Mama gives Naano a look I can tell means "Let it go."

Ever since I gave Jamal Mamoo and Nadia

Auntie a pep talk about taking control of their wedding, they've taken it, all right. Mamoo has a color-coded list on his laptop for each part of the wedding, including guests, vendors, and menu. There's still some grumbling and arguments, but Naano and Nadia's mom finally agreed to let them plan their own wedding. Mostly.

"What are these bags or boxes even for?" I ask. I'm sitting in the corner, elevating my foot on a stool. I'm wearing the "walking boot" that Dr. Alam gave me along with my crutches. It looks like a giant blue snow boot with the toes cut open and Velcro straps. My crutches are leaning against the wall near me.

"They're the goodie bags for the people who come to the wedding," Zara says. "We'll put them on the tables."

"What do you want inside? Nuts and dried

fruits? Chocolate?" Mama asks. "I vote for chocolate."

I expect Jamal Mamoo to agree. Instead, he shakes his head.

"Fortune cookies." He grins. "We're ordering custom ones with hilarious messages and little sayings about us on the inside."

"OH MY GOSH. THAT'S SO CUTE!" Zara gushes.

Even Naano nods her head in approval. She loves fortune cookies.

"What do you think, Skeletor?" Jamal Mamoo asks me.

"That's cool," I mumble. I feel slightly guilty that I'm not pretending to be more excited. But this wedding is all anyone is talking about, although it's still a month away.

Now I see Jamal Mamoo and Mama exchange a look.

"Come on, man," Jamal Mamoo says. "I need you to cheer up. I can't do this wedding thing without you. You're my best man."

"Yeah, Zayd," Zara chimes in. "You're in charge of the rings. And you have to dance at the mehndi." The pre-wedding party where everyone sings and dances is Zara's department, and she's planning every detail.

"I can't *dance!*" I remind everyone.

"Oh come on. You're not that bad of a dancer. I'll show you the moves. You can stand in the back," Zara says.

"I can't WALK properly!" I shout. "I can't RUN! Or JUMP! How am I supposed to DANCE?"

"Chill out, dude. I'm trying to help." Zara tosses her hair.

I can't help being grumpy. It's only been a couple of days since we saw the doctor, but I don't feel any better yet. Plus, I have basketball practice tomorrow, and Baba said I should still go to support my team despite my injury. If I don't get to play, I think I should at least get to chill at home and watch extra TV.

"You're going to be okay, Zayd." Jamal Mamoo comes over to me, picks up one of my crutches, and uses it to poke me. "Come on. I think we need to take a break from all this wedding stuff and play some 2K."

"Fine."

I know he's trying to cheer me up, as I hop down the stairs and settle into the couch. Naano for

sure is trying to make me feel better too when she sends Zara downstairs with a mango milkshake for me a little later. But even after Jamal Mamoo lets me win, and I drain the last drop of my milkshake, I only feel a tiny bit less lousy.

5

"Can I please help Zayd get to the lunchroom safely?" Adam asks Mr. Thomas. It's ten minutes before dismissal, and my best friend is using his extra-serious and responsible voice that he saves for teachers.

"I think he can manage by himself. Don't

you, Zayd?" Mr. Thomas raises his eyebrows at me as I stand up and fumble for my crutches. I have a note from the office giving me permission to leave class early to make my way down the halls before they get crowded. It ends up giving me an extra half hour of free time a day.

Adam pops up from his desk and hands me my crutches. He carefully tucks each one under my arms, and I hold on to the handles.

"I can't carry my lunch." I shrug, looking as helpless as I can.

"All right." Mr. Thomas sighs. "But no horsing around, boys. Head straight to the lunchroom."

"Yes, sir." Adam grins. He grabs my lunch and his own from our cubbies, and we stumble out of the room, bumping into desks, while everyone else stares at us, jealous.

"YES! Freedom!" Adam throws up his hands when we get into the hallway and he shuts the door behind us. "It's so great you're hurt."

I whack him, using one of my crutches.

"Is NOT."

"You know what I mean. Careful with the throwing arm." Adam rubs the side of his arm. Ever since he started playing football instead of basketball with me, he talks as if he's in the NFL or something. "Where should we go?"

"The lunchroom?"

"Let's go to the kindergarten wing. They might have cupcakes or donuts."

"Mr. Thomas said go straight to lunch," I say.

"We are going straight. The long way. Come on!"

The hallway is wide and empty, and I can swing freely on the crutches without bumping into anything.

"You're getting pretty good on those," Adam says.

"Yeah, I guess." I want to complain about how it's not fun at all and how I wish I could walk and play like normal.

"Can I try them?" he asks.

"Now?"

"Yeah. No one will see." Adam puts our lunches on the floor and reaches for the crutches.

"Okay."

I slip off the crutches, hand them to Adam, and lean against the wall. He takes off down the hall, but he's half skipping and using both of his legs.

"You're cheating!" I yell after him. "You need to keep one leg up the way I do."

A door pops open,

and my old kindergarten teacher, Ms. Riley, sticks her head out.

"What are you two doing? Where are you supposed to be?" she says. Her usual cheery face is scowling.

"Going to lunch," Adam pants. "We have a pass. He's hurt."

Ms. Riley looks down at my boot. Then she turns her gaze to Adam holding my crutches.

"That's no excuse for disturbing other classes. Get to the lunchroom before I write you a pink slip."

"Sorry," Adam mumbles.

"Feel better, Zayd," Ms. Riley says. She gives me a sympathetic half smile. We don't get cupcakes, but at least we don't get in trouble, either.

During recess, Adam has the brilliant idea to organize a crutches race. We keep time while

Blake, Chris, Adam, and I take turns hopping on the crutches from one end of the blacktop to the other. Chris is so much taller than me that he has to stoop to use the crutches. Blake is surprisingly quick. And Adam keeps track of everyone's times and whether they beat me.

"You smoked us all!" Adam high-fives me. "You're so fast!"

"That was awesome," Blake adds. "Let's do it again tomorrow."

I agree, and as I head back to class, I notice my crutches are all scratched up from falling on the asphalt so many times. I don't care, though, since I'm counting down the days until I can get rid of them and get back on the court.

6

"How many weeks did you say?" Coach Wheeler is looking at his clipboard at his starting lineup. He's tapping his pen the way he always does when he's thinking.

"Four. So I have three weeks and two days left," I say.

"Sorry to hear it. You in pain?"

"Not much anymore. I'm going to get checked in two weeks, and the doctor said I might be able to play sooner." Did Dr. Alam actually say that? Or am I just wishing he did? I'm not sure.

"We'll miss you. Don't rush it, though. Make sure you heal properly."

I look at Coach in surprise. He's always pushing us so hard, sweating on the sidelines, and yelling during our games. I thought he'd want me back as soon as possible.

"So, um. Who are you going to put in on point?"

"It'll have to be Sam." Coach is frowning at the clipboard.

"Sam?"

"Yeah. I think he'll do all right."

"Um. Okay."

Ravindu comes up behind me.

"Oh man! Did you do that when you fell at practice?"

"Yeah."

"How long are you out?"

"Like three or four weeks."

"That means you miss the rest of the season!"

"Yeah." Ravindu talks too much.

"But we're playing the Lightning again."

The Lightning. We played them twice last season. Their players come to games in training shirts and take them off during warm-ups, the way the Wizards do. The names of their plays, "isolation" and "four out," sound legit. Ours have silly names like "suns" and "horns." A lot of the kids on the Lightning are tall, and they behave as if they're being scouted every game. Their attitude intimidates everyone, and we were scared of them too. Until we finally figured out how to break their press and win last time we played them.

"We need you," Ravindu continues. "We can't beat them without you."

"Thanks," I say. Ravindu is all right.

I sit on the bench and watch my team doing layups. Coach Wheeler pulls Sam aside, and I can tell when he says Sam needs to take my spot. Sam starts to nod his head quickly, and I hear him say "Okay, Coach" as he glances at me a few times.

I suddenly feel hot and sweaty, and my foot starts to itch inside my boot. Grabbing my crutches, I go outside to wait for Mama to pick me up. I'm going to convince Baba that I don't need to be at practice again. I'll come back in three weeks and two days, unless I'm ready to play sooner.

7

"Ballay ballay!" everyone shouts.

"Ballay ballay, bai torr punjaaban di," the auntie sitting in the middle of the floor sings loudly. She's banging on the wooden part of a two-sided drum using a spoon. Another lady is playing the drum with her hands.

The room is packed with mostly women and girls. They are crammed around the drummer, clapping and singing songs I don't understand. Nadia Auntie is perched on some bedlike thing draped in colorful fabric.

"Ballay ballay," Zara joins in for the refrain. She's reading the words off a paper and claps every now and then, sitting close to Mama. Naano is seated on a chair on the side next to Nadia Auntie's mom. They smile and nod but aren't singing or clapping. Every few minutes Naano leans over and whispers to Nadia Auntie's mom, and they both giggle. I'm pretty sure Naano is making wisecracks.

We're in the basement of some friends of Nadia Auntie's family, who are hosting a dholki for Jamal Mamoo and Nadia Auntie. When Mama told us about it a few days ago, and explained how a dholki was a pre-mehndi, or a *practice* singing and dancing party, Baba and I exchanged a look of panic.

"Zayd and I don't have to go, right?" he said.

"You should be there to support Jamal," Mama argued. "They would want us all to come."

"I thought dholkis were only for ladies?"

"No. It depends on the host. And they invited everyone."

I could tell Baba knew it was a losing battle when he tried to use me as an excuse.

"What about Zayd's ankle? Shouldn't he be resting it?"

I put on an extra-pained expression to help him out.

"Zayd goes to school and manages. He'll be fine. We're all going."

And that settled it.

Mama picked out matching shalwar kameezes for Baba and me: a deep maroon top over white pants. She tried to get Nana Abu to wear the same thing as us. But when we picked him up, Nana Abu had forgotten and was wearing a black vest over a cream shalwar kameez. He still looked sharp, though. I'd look better if I didn't have to roll up one of my pant legs to wear my walking boot.

Now all the men are sitting upstairs in the living room talking about cricket scores, the Pakistani prime minister, and other stuff so boring it makes my brain hurt. Jamal Mamoo was ordered to arrive later, around dinnertime. I think it's weird he doesn't get to be at a party that's supposed to be for him for the whole time, but Mama said it was so he could make a grand entrance. She told mamoo she'd text him fifteen minutes before he should come. I decided hanging out downstairs was the best option until he gets here.

"Zayd!" An auntie runs into the room and finds me sitting near the stairs. She obviously doesn't notice the giant boot on my foot when she says, "Beta, go run and get your mom. Quickly!"

"What's wrong?" I ask. Her voice is strange.

"Your grandfather. He fainted."

"Is he okay?" I jump up, forgetting my ankle, and feel a shock of pain.

"I see your mom," the auntie says, ignoring me, and she starts to push through the ladies to get to Mama.

Mama gets up and dashes up the stairs, her face white. Zara grabs Naano and follows more slowly. I hop behind them as fast as I can. When I get to the living room, Nana Abu is sitting on a sofa, surrounded by people.

Someone tries to hand him a glass of water, and he shakes his head. Another person is wiping his head using a kitchen towel.

As Naano gets closer, the others move out of the way. When she reaches him, she puts her hand on his shoulder. They speak to each other in Urdu while Baba and Mama huddle together talking with Nadia's dad.

"What's going on?" I pull on Zara's arm.

"I don't know," she says. And we both move closer to our parents.

"We should take him to the hospital," Baba is saying. "He needs to be checked out."

"I agree," Mama says.

My stomach starts to twist and churn when I hear the word "hospital." I hope Nana Abu is going to be okay.

8

The hospital waiting room is small and crowded. I'm sitting next to Jamal Mamoo, and Zara is on his other side. We're both leaning on him.

Jamal Mamoo's wearing the fancy shalwar kameez for the dholki he never went to. Mama called to tell him to meet us at Suburban Hospital when we left. Everyone from the party was ready to follow us to the hospital, but Mama begged them not to come, including Nadia Auntie's family.

"You have all these guests here," she said. "Please stay and enjoy and keep my father in your prayers."

Naano and Mama are in Nana Abu's room, and Baba is pacing the hall. Jamal Mamoo bought us a bunch of chips and candy bars from the vending machine, but no one is interested in eating anything.

"Mamoo?" I interrupt while he's texting Nadia Auntie.

"What's up, Skeletor?"

"What does 'ballay ballay' mean?"

Jamal Mamoo chuckles.

"I have no idea," he admits. "I don't know

what any of those wedding songs are talking about. Even though the aunties love them."

I see Baba talking to a doctor in the hallway, and Jamal Mamoo jumps up to join them. After a few minutes they come back into the waiting room.

"How's Nana Abu?" Zara asks.

"Can he go home now?" I add.

"Not yet," Baba says. "Nana Abu had a . . . ah . . . minor heart attack."

"A . . . HEART . . . ATTACK?" Zara starts to wail.

"No, no, no, it wasn't serious. He's going to be okay. The doctor said it's a warning to take better care of himself." Mamoo rubs her shoulders while Zara tries to pull herself together.

"When can he go home?" I ask. There's a giant lump in my throat.

"He needs to have a small procedure

tomorrow morning. Then he'll be home soon, inshallah," Baba says.

"Can we see him?" Zara asks with a sniffle.

"Sure. He'll be happy to see you. Come on." Baba takes Zara by the hand.

I hesitate.

"Need help, Skeletor?" Jamal Mamoo asks. "Isn't it time to get rid of those crutches?"

"I'm okay," I say. I trail behind them down the hall to where the patient rooms are. Some of the doors are open, and I can see the bottom half of beds and people's feet. It makes my stomach churn again to imagine my grandfather lying there the same way.

"Here we are." Baba pushes open the door to room A32. I see Naano first, sitting on a chair by the bed. She has her scarf on her hair and is praying. A worn copy of the Quran is sitting next to her.

Zara rushes over to Nana Abu, whose eyes grow bigger when he sees us and he gives us a tiny wave. She takes his hand and grasps it inside her own.

"How are you feeling?" she asks in a hushed voice. "Does it hurt?"

"I feel fine," Nana Abu says. "They are taking good care of me here."

I don't move closer. Nana Abu looks so small in the big hospital bed and older than he usually does. He's wearing a hospital gown instead of his nice party outfit, and his gray hair is a mess. A clear tube sticking in his hand is attached to a bag hanging on a pole. A screen above the bed is displaying zigzagged lines. I know one of the lines is his heartbeat because of cartoons. My own heart tightens when I see it.

"Zayd?" Mama asks me. "Don't you want to say salaam to Nana Abu?"

"We're both broken now, eh, Zayd?" Nana Abu says, motioning for me to come closer.

I swallow hard as I inch forward. The lump in my throat is growing bigger. If I try to speak, I'm going to start bawling. Jamal Mamoo is watching me closely, and he suddenly cuts in front of me.

"Abu, you saved me from being forced to dance in front of the aunties," Jamal Mamoo says extra loudly. "But seriously? A heart attack? You could have faked a fever or something."

Nana Abu starts to laugh.

Jamal Mamoo looks around. "I'm starving. Is there any real food in here? Did anyone pack up some food from the party for the handsome groom-to-be?"

Naano looks up from her prayer.

"Did they?" she asks. "I want biryani."

"Me too," Jamal Mamoo agrees. "I'm going to ask Nadia to bring some over right now."

"And some dessert!" Zara adds.

"Can she bring the drum, too?" I pipe up, finally able to speak.

Jamal Mamoo winks at me.

"Good idea," he says. "Let's bring the party in here. I'm sure the nurses won't mind."

Nana Abu's face breaks into a slow smile as I move forward to give him a hug.

9

"All right, let's do this!" I say.

Nana Abu is sitting on the recliner and resting his legs on a small stool next to Zara.

"You remember what the physical therapist said, right?" Zara asks him.

"Yes." Nana Abu grimaces.

"Okay, let's do the leg raises first."

She pulls the stool out of the way so Nana Abu can lift each leg up and down ten times.

"Look at me, Nana Abu," I say. "I have to do my exercises too."

Ever since Nana Abu got out of the hospital last week, he and Naano have been staying at our house. Mama said it would be easier for everyone to chip in and help take care of him. I think she also wants to have him near us. We all do.

It seems as if Nana Abu is moving in slow motion, although he's moving at his normal pace.

"One . . . two . . . three . . . ," he counts in a raspy breath.

"One . . . two . . . three . . . ," I say, rotating my ankle as I stick out my leg.

I went back to see Dr. Alam yesterday, and he said I'm healing well. I don't have to wear the boot or use the crutches anymore. He gave me some stretches to do and said I can start to put weight on my foot and try to walk normally. That was the good news. The bad news is I still can't run or jump for two more weeks.

"Aren't you guys cute," Mama says as she walks into the room. "I knew getting the kids to work with you on your exercises was a good idea."

"After this we have to walk around the house three times," Zara says to Nana Abu. "You have to get in your steps."

"Maybe later." Nana Abu smiles.

"He should rest," Naano says as she shuffles into the room behind Mama. "You people need to leave him alone."

"He's been resting all day," Mama argues. "The exercises are important for his recovery. It wouldn't hurt you to do them too, you know."

It's weird to see Mama bossing around the oldest people in the house. I can't imagine telling my parents what to do, or them listening to me.

But Naano wins. Until we sit down for dinner.

"What is this?" she asks, wearing a frown as Mama puts out a big bowl of salad. "Where's the food?"

"Salad is food," Mama says.

"Salad is what food eats," Naano mutters. Everyone laughs except for Mama. Well, Baba kind of cough-laughs into his napkin.

"I have grilled chicken breast and steamed broccoli, too. After the salad. We need to eat more veggies and cut down on salt for heart health, right?" Mama stares at all of us.

"I love salad," Zara says smugly as she scoops some onto her plate.

Naano gives me a gigantic eye roll. I could kiss her.

Every meal has been similar to this for the past few days. Naano asks for salt and butter and Mama refuses, arguing that in her house they have to eat her food. Naano threatens to leave or to smuggle in parathas and extra-greasy halwa. Mama tries to ignore Naano, while we secretly give her thumbs up.

The best part of the bickering is watching Nana Abu smile through it all. It might be because he isn't wearing his hearing aid. But I think it's because he's happy to be home. I'm happy we get to do our exercises and complain about healthy food together. Later I might try to sneak us some ice cream.

10

I'm in the middle of naming my avatar in NBA 2K Wizzy the Wall-rus after my favorite basketball player, John Wall, when Baba yells from upstairs.

"Zayd! We're leaving in five minutes. Where are you?"

"Do I *have* to go?"

"Excuse me? Are you yelling to me from downstairs? Get up here."

I turn off the game and drag my feet up the stairs slowly. Not because my ankle hurts—because it doesn't. I'm just not in a hurry to leave.

"I don't want to go to the game if I'm not playing, Baba. Please?" I don't add how going to practice was miserable. I missed the last couple of practices and games because of Nana Abu getting sick. Now, since life is mostly back to normal, Baba is forcing me to go to the last game of the season. My team has to win to make the playoffs.

"We already talked about this." Baba frowns.

"Yeah, but . . ." I pause. "You don't know how horrible it feels to sit there and watch and not play."

Baba runs his hand through his hair and pauses before speaking.

"You remember when John Wall hurt his knee, right?" he asks.

"Yeah."

"Wasn't he there, for every game? Cheering on his teammates?"

"Yeah."

"And wasn't he still a leader?"

"I guess so."

"And isn't he your favorite player?"

"Yeah." I don't mention I was just naming my avatar after him.

"So get dressed already. Come on. No arguments."

"What should I wear? A suit and tie?" I figure if Baba wants me to imitate John Wall, I might as well go all the way.

"If you want. Whatever you wear, brush your teeth, please. There's some serious stench coming out of your face."

I put on an old basketball camp T-shirt and shorts and quickly brush my teeth. On the drive to the game, I think about what Baba said. John Wall is my favorite player in the NBA. Ever since I've been playing point guard, I've been watching his moves extra closely. I love the way he plays with heart and passion. And I suppose he's always there for his team.

But he also gets paid millions of dollars. He gets to be on TV. He doesn't have to go to school. There aren't thousands of fans waiting for me to arrive at the game. Plus, there aren't any cameras around, unless you count Chris's mom, who brings a gigantic lens to every game and takes a million pictures of her kid.

"Hey, Zayd," Coach Wheeler says as we walk into the gym. "Good to see you. How's the ankle?"

"Getting better," I say. "I should be back soon."

I start to follow Baba up the bleachers, but Coach points to the bench.

"Sit with the team."

I do what I'm told. Everyone else says "hey" to me when they come back to the bench after shooting around. As they crowd around Coach for the pregame pep talk, I stand awkwardly to one side.

"Zayd's going to take us out." Coach surprises me when he's done speaking.

Everyone opens up the circle, and I step forward to put my hand in the middle like I usually do for games.

"One two three . . . ," I say.

"MD HOOPS!" everyone shouts.

I look back at Baba, and he smiles at me from the bleachers. It does feel kind of good to be here. When I smile back at Baba, he knows I'm admitting it.

11

Coach Wheeler asks me to stand next to him during the game. Actually, he doesn't stand a whole lot. During all our games, he paces the sidelines and motions and sweats a bunch.

"Great rebounding!" he yells.

I can't keep up with him since I've just started walking normally again. So I stay in one place. But he keeps coming up to me and commenting on the game like I'm an assistant coach or something. I realize I never got to ask him about being the new team captain after I got hurt. Right now doesn't seem like the right time.

"We need to keep shooting while we're hot," Coach mumbles to me. I agree. Our team is on a run.

I felt a twinge of jealousy when Sam started the game at point guard instead of me. Now, a few minutes into the game, I can tell he's been working on his skills. He's moving the ball really well. We need to win to clinch our playoff spot, so everyone has to play their best, including Sam.

But if Sam plays *really* well, will Coach keep

him in my spot when I'm better? What if he picks him to be the new team captain?

"Subs!" Coach yells, and he puts in a couple of second-string players. Sam is still in the game, and my eyes are glued on him as I wonder what I would do if I was playing in his place. I notice all the good things he does. He has an awesome assist and a smooth no-look pass. I also see him rush a shot when he had time and flub his crossover.

One thing stands out on offense. Whenever a defender rushes at Sam, he looks to his right and passes to Blake on that side. A couple of times Blake had someone covering him tight, and he lost the ball. Meanwhile, Matthew was wide open on the left side of the basket.

This happens three different times, and the third time, the defender is anticipating Sam's pass and blocks it. It's right before halftime, and I'm sure Coach is going to point it out during the break. Instead he talks about other things, including everyone's energy level and remembering not to reach in on defense.

"We're up by eight," Coach wraps up. "But don't get fooled by the score. They're outhustling us, and we could be doing better. We need to finish strong if we want to do well in the playoffs. Let's give it our all this second half."

Coach has Sam take everyone out this time. I know I already had my turn at the beginning of the game. But it still stings a little bit.

Sam walks by me to put his water bottle back on the bench. I hesitate for a second, wondering what to do.

"Hey, Sam," I finally say.

"Hey." Sam looks at me.

"Good game so far."

"Thanks." Sam smiles and takes a sip of his water.

"I . . . um . . ."

I pause, wondering if I should say something about his passing or not. If Coach didn't say anything to him, why should I? He probably won't want to hear it from me. Besides, we're winning anyway.

"Yeah?" Sam looks at me and then at the court. It's time to go back on.

"Nice handles."

"Thanks." Sam's smile grows bigger.

During the second half, I try to squash the feeling of jealousy whenever Coach praises Sam. I make sure to yell extra loudly for everyone else on the team when they do something well. We pull out the win, and everyone is grinning at the end of the game. I'm happy too, because it means our season isn't over. But I down look at my foot and pray it's better in time for me to return for the playoffs. I'm dying to get back in the game.

12

"No, no, no, not that way. This way." Aliya, Mama's friend's daughter, hops as she flicks out her hand.

A line of girls, including Zara, are standing behind her and trying to mimic her actions. It's not working, and they're all doing the moves at different times.

"Okay, now show me." Aliya turns around and watches them. She doesn't say anything as she watches but kind of groans.

"Let's skip to the next part. We're going to be in a line. Move your hands like this." Aliya demonstrates.

A group of kids are crowded into our family room, where the coffee table is pushed out of the way. We're practicing dances for Jamal Mamoo's mehndi, which is on Friday night, only three days away. Zara insists we need at least three planned dances, based on the last one of these singing-and-dancing henna parties we went to. I don't think she remembers how the people at those parties could have easily been professional Bollywood dancers, not a bunch of kids who've never danced desi style before.

The worst part is the first dance is a cheesy love song. Zara thought it would be cute to include it. Aliya is the only one who speaks Urdu and understands what it's saying, so she's in charge of deciding the steps.

"At this part, when it says 'you're my heart and my life,' put your hands over your heart and make it thump like this."

Zara and the other girls look at one another. I wonder if Zara is thinking it's a mistake to have Aliya call the shots. I do. I watch while Zara nods her head and goes along and copies the moves. THUMP. THUMP. THUMP. It looks ridiculous.

Aliya's younger brother, Sulaiman, is the only guy who is almost as into dancing as she is. He doesn't seem to mind prancing around and pretending to be one of the dudes in love who act like fools in Naano's favorite Pakistani dramas. But he's seven.

Musa, a seventh grader who was probably dragged here by his parents, is sitting on the side next to me, watching with eyebrows raised.

"I'm not doing that," he says.

"Me neither," I agree. "I can't jump around. Doctor's orders."

"You can walk, Zayd," Aliya says. "But Sulaiman and Musa, you two jump."

"Not happening," Musa says.

Sulaiman looks slightly disappointed but says, "Yeah, let's do something else."

"We already agreed on this!" Aliya throws up her hands. "Do YOU have any better ideas?"

"How about we do a mash-up of songs?" I suggest. The idea just pops into my head. "We can use some of Jamal Mamoo's favorite hip-hop songs and mix them with Bollywood. What are those old-school movies he said he watched with Naano when he was a kid?"

Zara looks doubtful at first but then starts to get excited.

"I know a good mash-up app!" she says.

"Wait, wait. What about THIS dance?" Aliya glares at everyone. "We already worked so hard on it. I have all the steps done."

"I think this will be easier, and Jamal Mamoo will love it. We can do one big mash-up song instead of three different ones and be done," Zara soothes. "Is that okay?"

"Fine." Aliya doesn't look happy about it at all.

I get to work picking out the songs. I throw in "Heart of the City" by Jay-Z, since we always listen to it when we play 2K, and a bunch of my uncle's other favorites. Zara runs upstairs to ask Mama for the names of old Bollywood songs they listened to as kids. Within an hour

we have a professional-sounding mash-up. Aliya finally gets into it too.

Next comes the dancing part. Somehow I end up being the one in charge, probably since I'm the one not dancing. I throw up some music videos on Zara's tablet and piece together a dance, picking out the coolest moves from each clip. Surprisingly, it feels like I'm coaching and designing basketball plays.

Except the plays involve people jumping past one another instead of making jump shots and spinning around in a circle instead of trying a spin move to the hoop. Either way, everyone listens to me, and it actually comes together.

"My legs hurt," a girl named Fatima complains after we've been at it for another hour.

"I need water," Musa says. He wipes sweat off his brow.

"Okay, how about a fifteen-minute water break before we do it one more time," I suggest. "Let's give it our all until the end of practice."

As the words come out of my mouth, they sound familiar. I suddenly realize exactly who I sound like: Coach Wheeler! I can live with that. If I'm half as good of a coach as he is, this dance is going to be epic.

13

"Come on, Abu, please?" Mama is leaning over Nana Abu, who is sitting in his favorite chair.

"Maybe later," Nana Abu mumbles.

"But you didn't do it yesterday, either. The doctor says—"

"I will later." Nana Abu cuts Mama off. He

settles back into the recliner, pulls a throw blanket up to his chin, and falls asleep.

Mama looks at me and sighs as she walks into the kitchen.

"I'm worried about him," she whispers.

"What's the matter?" I feel dread spreading inside me. "Is Nana Abu sick again?"

"No. But he's not motivated to exercise. He hasn't showered, and he's sitting around in his pajamas. It's not like him."

"Maybe he's tired," I say.

"I know, but the doctor said it's important for him to keep moving."

"Is he going to be okay?" I ask.

Mama looks at me and forces a smile.

"Of course he is, sweetie. You're right. He's probably just tired. You want a snack?"

"No thanks."

Mama starts rummaging through the fridge,

but I head back into the family room and watch Nana Abu snoozing for a few minutes. I suddenly have an idea and go upstairs to look for Zara. She's in her room wearing headphones and doesn't hear me until I'm almost yelling her name.

"WHAT?" she yells back.

"I. NEED. YOUR. HELP."

Zara frees one of her ears. "I'm busy," she says.

"It's for Nana Abu," I add.

That works. Zara gives me her full attention while I tell her my plan. We head to the garage and start to search through boxes of junk.

"Here it is!" I hold up a dust-covered bat. This isn't any old bat. It's a cricket bat Nana Abu used to play with on his team when he was young in Pakistan. He gave it to Baba ages ago, but no one has used it in years.

"Nana Abu!" Zara and I race into the family room. "We need you!"

"What is it?" Nana Abu opens his eyes slowly.

"I'm trying to show Zara how to bowl, but she's doing it all wrong. She says she's right. But I know I am!" I hold up the bat.

"You're playing *cricket*?" Nana Abu is fully awake now.

"Yeah. I know all the rules from watching matches at your house. Zara and I want to play. Can you help us?"

In cricket, which is similar to baseball, bowling is the same as pitching, except you hit the ground with the ball and make it bounce. Cricket players hold the bat upside down, and there are things called wickets instead of bases. Players go back and forth between two wickets and can score hundreds of runs in a game.

"I was captain of my cricket team," Nana Abu says, not moving.

"I know." Zara tugs on his blanket. "That's why we need you to teach us. Please?"

"Where?" Nana Abu looks reluctant.

"Right outside."

"Well okay. I have to change my clothes." Nana Abu gets out of the chair and shuffles to the guest room. Ten minutes later he returns in a tracksuit.

We head outside to the lawn.

"Watch this," Zara says. She runs as fast as she can and hurls a tennis ball into the grass about two feet in front of me. I'm standing, holding the bat the way I would position a hockey stick. The ball rolls to my feet and stops.

"No, no, this won't do." Nana Abu shakes his head. "We need a hard surface."

"Can we go down to the little park and play

on the basketball court?" Zara suggests.

"Yes, all right," Nana Abu agrees. "But first show me the ball."

I hand Nana Abu the tennis ball, and he grips it in his right hand.

"See how my fingers are? Try holding the ball like this. And the most important thing is your follow-through."

"Like in basketball?" I ask.

"Yes."

As we walk to the park, Zara gives me a secret high five. We got Nana Abu to change his clothes and exercise! And he didn't even realize it because he was playing his favorite sport. Even though I still prefer basketball, cricket might be my second favorite. Especially if I get to play with my grandfather.

14

"We're on next," Zara announces. Her pink outfit is sparkly, and she's wearing a jeweled clip in her hair.

We're gathered around a dance floor in front of the small stage at the mehndi where Jamal Mamoo and Nadia Auntie sit on a carved bench swing. Red, gold, and dark green curtains are hanging behind them. Their fancy ,outfits match the colors of the decorations. Low tables filled with candles and trays of henna are arranged around their feet.

"Actually the aunties want to go next," Zara says as a bunch of older ladies get up and crowd the dance floor. I watch as they tug on Naano's hand, trying to get her to join them. She shakes her head and crosses her arms. Naano doesn't dance.

The deejay plays some song I don't recognize, and the aunties form a big circle. I can't help but think of basketball, the way they all put their hands together in the middle like my team does. Except they pull their hands up and put them back in again over and over. In between, they snap and clap and touch their elbows as they dance around. The thought of my team doing that makes me smile.

"They didn't practice," Aliya whispers to us. "They're so out of sync."

"They're aunties." Zara shrugs. "They're having fun."

Everyone claps politely for them when they finish, but they don't seem to notice. They are too busy congratulating themselves. Next it's our turn.

"Come on, everybody!" Zara says. Everyone gets in position, and I give the deejay the signal to start.

I'm nervous we won't be able to pull it off and worry everyone will forget the moves or the order of the songs. Every time a new part of the mash-up begins, someone has to use a prop—a pair of sunglasses or a wig or a scarf. When you add in the dance moves, it's a lot to keep track of. My job is to coach, and I only have a small part where I do a goofy walk into the middle of the dance floor wearing a hat over my eyes.

The music begins, and everyone is perfect to start. As in they are seriously killing it! I'm proud of them and steal a look at Jamal Mamoo and Nadia Auntie. They are clapping and cheering.

The grand finale is a Hindi song called "It's the Time to Disco" that has some English lines in it. We bust out some ridiculous moves that make Jamal Mamoo start to cry from laughing so hard. Then, as the last song ends, I run up and grab him and Nadia Auntie from the stage and pull them onto the dance floor.

"That was AMAZING!" Jamal Mamoo yells to me over the music. "I'm so impressed. Thank you guys for doing that!"

I grin at him. We pulled it off! Jamal

Mamoo and Nadia Auntie start to sway to the music. Suddenly mamoo's friends sneak up from behind and pick him up by the legs. He puts his arms in the air and waves his hands around as everyone hoots.

I see Jamal Mamoo point at me, and—WHOA!—the next thing I know I'm being

hoisted up onto some big dude's shoulders. I have no idea what to do, so I stick my hands up the way mamoo does and try not to fall off.

Zara runs over to Nana Abu and pulls him off his seat, and they dance together. Naano actually gets up too, and the two of them hold one of Zara's hands each and laugh while they slowly move to the beat. When I get back down to the dance floor, everyone boogies their hearts out. I manage to hop around a little, and my ankle doesn't hurt.

"I think I can play tomorrow!" I yell to Baba, pointing to my ankle. Tomorrow's our first playoff game. "Dr. Alam said I can play when I feel ready."

He gives me an "okay" sign while he does an awkward Punjabi dance move, acting like he's screwing in an imaginary lightbulb.

"We're going to do the traditions now, so

come on up and let's see how much mithai we can feed these guys!" the deejay announces.

Jamal Mamoo and Nadia Auntie settle back on the bench swing. Mamoo wipes the sweat off his forehead using a big dinner napkin while everyone crowds around them. The aunties place a dab of henna paste onto a big leaf on their hands and offer their congratulations. We all watch as they take turns feeding them Pakistani sweets. Jamal Mamoo obediently opens his mouth each time, even when the giggling ladies try to cram in huge pieces of mithai.

"Help me, Zayd!" he begs. "I'm going to gag." I stand next to him and convince the aunties to feed him M&M's instead.

After the rituals are over, it's time for family photos. Mama and Baba and Naano and Nana Abu come up to the stage and sit on either side of the bride and groom. Zara and I kneel in front. Nadia's parents come up too. Next her aunts and uncles and cousins and others I don't know join the crowd. It feels like a hundred people are squeezed onto the stage.

After my face hurts from smiling for pictures, I escape with Zara back to the buffet area to get a drink and some more of my favorite butter chicken. Dancing made me hungry. The food is already gone, but there's a bunch of desserts spread out on the tables now. SCORE! Along with mithai and rice pudding, there are plenty of cupcakes, too. When Jamal Mamoo and Nadia Auntie went to taste wedding cakes, they couldn't decide on a flavor, so they decided to get them all in cupcake form. Genius.

I devour a chocolate caramel cupcake and half of Zara's white chocolate raspberry one. I can't decide which one is better. Between the food, dancing, and seeing everyone so happy, this night was incredible. Plus, I'm finally ready to play.

15

I throw on my basketball uniform and strap on my high-tops. The Jordans Jamal Mamoo gave me when I first made the gold team feel as good as ever. I've kept them clean, so they look almost new.

"How you feeling?" Baba asks. He looks

tired. We got home late last night after the mehndi finally ended, and it's only eight a.m. I had a hard time waking up too. Mama and Zara are sleeping, so we crept around downstairs and ate cereal as quietly as we could.

"Pretty good," I say. I hop up and down a few times to test out my ankle. "Like normal."

"All right, great." Baba grabs a hat to cover his bedhead, and we get in the car. My stomach starts to clench a little, the way it always does when I'm nervous. I wonder what Coach is going to do about letting me play. I've been out for four weeks and missed practice and the last four games. Will he still start me in our first playoff game? I hope so.

Everyone looks as nervous as I feel when we gather around Coach for a pregame talk. The Badgers are a team we haven't played before, so we don't know anything about them.

"Okay, boys, I need everyone to play smart. You've worked hard all season, and it comes down to this," Coach says. "If we win this game, we're in the championship."

Then he gives us the starting lineup. I hold my breath, and . . . he says he's putting in Sam as starting point guard. I bite my lip.

"Zayd, you'll sub in for Sam. You let me know how you feel. Okay?"

"Sure, Coach. I feel good," I say, trying not to show disappointment on my face.

I start the game sitting on the bench, so I focus on figuring out the other team. They've got a couple of enormous kids, and their point guard is quick. But they look beatable.

In the first minute of the game, Sam makes a sweet move and passes the ball to Blake for a jumper. It's good! A few seconds later Matthew steals the ball from one of the tall kids, takes it down on a fast break, and makes an easy layup. I'm itching to get in the game and keep looking at the game clock.

After the first four minutes, we're up 6–4. Coach finally calls for subs, and I literally leap off the bench. Sam slaps my hand as he jogs off the court. Ravindu inbounds the ball, and I start to work my way to half court.

It feels great to be back in the game. But as I dribble, I suddenly become extra aware of my ankle. It doesn't hurt or anything. I just keep picturing my X-ray and the drawing of the ligaments inside my leg as I move. What if my ankle isn't fully healed? What if I twist it when I make a cut? What if I fall again?

I see a lane where I could drive to the hoop but pass the ball to Blake instead. He takes a jump shot and bricks it. Coach grimaces a little, but he doesn't say anything.

The Badgers score on their next possession. We're tied now. I get the ball back and pass it to Ravindu when a defender approaches me as soon as we cross half court. He takes a shot from close to the three-point line and airballs it. The ball rolls out of bounds, and I hear Coach yelling for a time out.

"Sam, you're back in," Coach says. "Ravindu, don't rush your shots. You guys need to calm down."

The whistle blows, and I head to the bench, but Coach stops me.

"What's up? Your ankle bothering you?"

"No," I say. "Not really."

"You're hesitating and playing timid. We can't afford for you not to give a hundred percent right now. You understand, right?"

"Yes, Coach."

"Let me know when you're ready go back in," Coach says.

I sit down and feel my face burn a little. I thought I was ready to play. I *am* ready! Although as I watch Sam hustle up and down the court, I notice how he goes all out when he runs. He doesn't seem to think about getting hurt the way he dives for the ball after an attempted steal pops it loose. I have to admit it reminds me of the way John Wall will do anything to make a play.

Right before the half ends, I notice Sam does the same thing as last game: He passes to Blake on the right and misses an opportunity to find Matthew open on the other side. We're down by two and are in a must-win situation. So this time I decide to speak up during halftime.

"Hey, Sam." I tap his arm and take a deep

breath. "Listen. I . . . um . . . noticed you pass a lot to Blake on the elbow."

"Yeah?" Sam squints his eyes, waiting for me to continue.

"And Matthew was open on the left. So try to look to for him, too, if you can."

Sam frowns slightly.

"Okay." He finally nods. "I didn't see him."

I notice that during the second half he takes my advice and doesn't make the same mistake again. It feels good to make a difference. I finally go back in and play better than I did in the first half. I make a good assist and one shot off the backboard.

Blake throws up a fist as the buzzer sounds.

We win 33–29 and are in the championship finals!

As we celebrate, Sam gives me a big high five. Coach pats me on the back.

"It's good to have you back, Zayd," he says.

"I like the leadership you're demonstrating."

I wonder if Coach overheard me talk to Sam. Maybe it will help convince him I should be team captain next season.

I won't lie: It feels really good to be back, and I'm glad I helped my team out. In the finals, though, I have to do better, a whole lot better. If I'm supposed to lead my team, I need to find a way to put my injury behind me and truly bounce back.

16

Adam's mom cries about everything. I've seen her cry during diaper commercials. She cried when she picked us up on the last day of school last year. Somehow she even managed to cry during our end-of-season party when Adam was still on my basketball team.

My mom? She's the opposite of Adam's mom. It takes a lot to make her cry. It takes even more for Naano to shed a tear. Today, the day of Jamal Mamoo's wedding, they are both crying buckets. It's kind of freaking me out.

It started this morning when we had breakfast and talked about the mehndi on Friday.

"I can't believe you and Abu danced together," Mama said, sniffling. "It was the most beautiful thing I've ever seen."

"Well, who knows how long we have left, right?" Naano joked, jabbing her elbow into Nana Abu's side. "We might as well dance for the first times in our lives."

She was kidding, but it made Mama cry harder. Naano's eyes filled up too. Then Jamal Mamoo, who was getting dressed for the wedding at our house, came out in his groom's outfit, and the tears started flowing again.

"Don't laugh, Skeletor," mamoo warned. He was wearing a long, stiff, embroidered jacket and white pants with gold threads on the edges. Best of all, he had on slippers that curled up in the front like a genie's lamp while he gave me an "I dare you to make fun of me" stare.

"You're a prince!" Mama exclaimed between sniffs. As corny as it sounds, I had to agree.

"Or a king, Mamoo," I said. "For real. I dig the shoes."

And now we're lined up to enter into the wedding hall, where the imam is waiting to perform the marriage ceremony. Mama is fixing the flower that's pinned on Nana Abu's jacket and wiping her eyes at the same time. Nana Abu looks handsome, like an older, grayer, less fancy version of Jamal Mamoo. I never noticed before how much they look alike.

We wait for Nadia's cousin to announce us over the microphone, and file in as all the guests watch. Zara and I are first up. I manage to get down the aisle without tripping while Zara practically skips. Mama and Baba are next, holding hands and blushing. And then King Mamoo walks in, standing extra tall, with Naano and Nana Abu on either side of him. He heads over to the decorated stage, where the imam is standing. They hug and turn to wait for Nadia's family to enter.

A couple of little girls throw flower petals on the ground, and then the bride makes a grand entrance. Everyone in the crowd stands up and murmurs their approval. She's a sparkling queen in cream and gold, the perfect other half to Jamal Mamoo. I see Mama wiping her eyes again as Nadia Auntie takes her place on the stage next to mamoo.

"Asalaamualaikum." The imam starts speaking. He talks about the beauty of marriage in Islam and the meaning of love, and asks each person in the room to ask for blessings for the marriage. When he finishes, everyone in the audience says "ameen" in one voice.

I try not to fidget on the stage as I wait until it's time for my job—handing Jamal Mamoo a ring. He takes it, says a few words, and puts the ring on Nadia Auntie's hand. She does the same in return. Then we stand there and wait and . . . nothing happens.

"Dude, aren't you supposed to, like, kiss the bride?" I whisper to Jamal Mamoo. At least I think I'm whispering. I guess I'm louder than I meant to be. Or maybe everyone else is super quiet. Jamal Mamoo turns red and lets out his wacky laugh. Nadia Auntie starts to giggle. Soon everyone starts cracking up. I'm not sure why, because I'm completely serious.

"How about they . . . ahem . . . celebrate in private later," the imam says with a chuckle. "But in the meantime, everyone please join me in congratulating the new couple!"

Jamal Mamoo takes Nadia Auntie by the hand, and they walk out of the room while everyone stands and cheers. We all go into a long hallway and eat tiny samosas and chicken pakoras passed around by waiters in tuxedos. Finally we go into a big ballroom, where round tables are set up with the gold fortune cookie boxes on everyone's plates. There's a long table on a stage set up for the bride and groom and their families, including Zara and me.

"Zayd, what were you thinking?" Mama exclaims when she corners me in the ballroom. "Have you seen kissing at other Pakistani weddings?"

"I guess not. I was thinking of TV weddings."

"This is a little different. And besides, Naano and Nana Abu would totally flip out," she adds.

"Yeah. I didn't think about what all the old people would think," I say.

We both pause, imagining. Then Mama starts to laugh and pulls me into a big hug. I see tears in her eyes, but they are the happy kind.

"I love you. Isn't this a wonderful day?" she says, looking over at her father. "I'm so grateful we could all be here together. And now I finally have a sister."

I give her a quick hug back and don't say anything because her words make me tear up too. In a good way. But just a tiny bit.

17

"Oh man, our worst nightmare. It's the Lightning," Ravindu groans as we walk into the gym together for our final game of the season: the championship!

"Are you surprised?" I ask. The Lightning are fierce. They always make it to the finals.

"No." Ravindu frowns. "But I wish it were someone else."

"We've beaten them," I remind him.

"I know." Ravindu still looks worried as he eyes the team warming up in their training shirts. I hide the fact that my insides are doing little flips and that I wish we were playing anyone else but these guys too.

"Good luck," Zara says. She gives me a fist bump and heads to the bleachers with my parents. Naano and Nana Abu made it out for the game too. Mama had tried to tell Nana Abu they didn't have to come since the bleachers would be uncomfortable.

"No," he'd said. "I'm going to see my grandson be a champion."

And now he takes a seat near the front, in his tracksuit and aviator sunglasses. He's the essence of cool. Jamal Mamoo wanted to come too, but he and Nadia Auntie left early this morning for their honeymoon in Florida. He texted Mama to wish me good luck and sent a million emojis of basketballs and trophies and a guy surfing, who I guess is supposed to be him.

Adam's already here, sitting next to his dad. He's wearing his old MD Hoops jersey, and it means a lot to have him here. My nerves kick into high gear when I think of everyone who came out to watch me. I have my own little cheering section on the bleachers.

"Zayd!" Coach calls me over to him. "How you feeling?"

"Good."

"Think you can start?"

"Yes, Coach!"

YES!

"I need you bring it strong. Can you do that?"

"Yes, Coach." I wonder if he can hear my heart pounding.

"Okay, let's do this."

Coach calls us all into a huddle.

"This is it, guys. This is the championship. You guys worked hard this season, overcoming injury . . ."

Everyone looks at me when he says that.

". . . and stepping up when you were needed . . ."

Everyone looks at Sam when he says that.

". . . and playing with your heart and your heads. I'm proud of you, no matter what happens in this game. Although I know you can win this. Focus and play smart. Are you with me?"

"Yes, Coach!" we all say.

"Zayd, take us out," Coach says.

We put our hands together.

"We got this!" I say. "One two three . . ."

"MD HOOPS!" everyone yells.

"Good luck," Sam says to me as we walk onto the court.

"You too," I reply.

"How's your ankle?" Sam asks.

"All better," I say. I'm not just saying it. I mean it. This morning I was up early, doing drills and shooting free throws on my driveway, and it felt perfect.

Coach is starting Sam at shooting guard. We haven't played together in a while. Today we need to be in sync and unstoppable, the way John Wall and Bradley Beal are when they find their rhythm.

I look around at Blake, Ravindu, and Matthew before sizing up the other team as we warm up. They are gigantic—like they each grew an inch since the last time we played them. Their point guard has a scowl on his face that resembles a cartoon villain so much it's almost funny.

I try to ignore how big they are and how good I know they are. Instead, I focus on the game as the buzzer sounds and we get ready for tip-off.

18

THWACK!

Number seven on the Lightning smacks the ball as I hold it up to make a pass. I'm being smothered by the defense. I manage to get the ball away and make a high pass to Blake. He dribbles and gets the ball to Matthew on the inside. I hold my breath as Matthew backs into a defender and turns to make a jump shot. It hits the rim and . . . it goes in!

We're down by one point, and the score has been up and down for the first seven minutes. Coach's shirt is already soaked in sweat, and he has been yelling nonstop. We're trying to keep up, but the Lightning are hot.

"It's too close," Sam says as we run back to defend.

I look at Coach to see what he signals. He's motioning for us to press harder. These guys are scoring no matter what we do on defense.

We double-team their gigantic point guard, but he burns us with his crossover. He gets the ball down to his power forward, who puts it in for an easy layup.

Coach calls time out.

"Okay, forget the press. Stick to the two-three zone. Zayd, you have to protect the ball while it's in your hands. Don't give them any chance to steal."

The referee blows the whistle, and we run back onto the court. I move the ball, looking for an opportunity to score. I've missed two shots already and haven't put up any points. It's already nine minutes into the half. I can't go scoreless!

I get past my defender, and Sam dishes the ball to me for an open pull-up jumper right inside the three-point line. It hits the rim and bounces right into the raised hands of the tallest kid on the Lightning.

ARGH! What's going on?

In the next three minutes the Lightning score twice. We turn the ball over once and get fouled. Ravindu goes to the line and makes one and misses one.

I'm shocked by how fast time is going by when the buzzer sounds at the end of the first half. We're down by six, and the Lightning lead. I can't believe I haven't scored. This is not at all how I imagined my return.

We all huddle around Coach, panting and chugging water.

"You're still in this," he says. "Don't let being down get to you."

I gulp some water and turn my head to the stands to where my family is sitting. Mama and Zara wave at me. Baba looks totally stressed out. Naano is talking to the lady next to her. Nana Abu has taken off his sunglasses. He catches my eye, raises his arm, and makes a fist.

Last night, when I said good night to Nana Abu, he pulled me close to him.

"You know, Zayd, when I was captain of my cricket team, we played in our championship tournament. I was very nervous about the other team. My father said something to me I never forgot," he said. I waited as he fell silent, lost in his thoughts.

"What did he say?" I asked after a few moments.

"What was I saying?"

"What your father said, before the championship game?"

"Ah yes." Nana Abu smiled. "Your great grandfather said, 'Don't let what you *can't* do get in the way of what you *can* do.'"

I didn't know what he was talking about and only pretended to agree that it was amazing advice. Now I think I finally understand what he meant.

I turn my attention back to Coach. As soon as he finishes speaking, Adam stands up and yells from the bleachers.

"LET'S GO, GOLD!"

Everyone cheers and gets fired up. Coach has Ravindu take us out. I can tell Ravindu's still nervous, because his voice squeaks as he counts, "One two three . . ."

"MD HOOPS!" I shout. I glance up into the stands again. Mama and Zara give me thumbs up. Baba points at me and yells, "Go, Zayd!" Naano is still talking to the lady next to her. Nana Abu gives me a knowing look.

I nod back at him and jump up and down a few times to get myself pumped before I run onto the court.

19

We start the second half with the ball. I call for a screen. Matthew runs over to set the pick and creates an opening in the lane. I take a step, pull up, and miss the shot.

"Don't rush, Zayd!" Coach yells from the sideline. I don't look at him, because I know I could have set that up better. My shot is still off, and I feel myself starting to panic.

The Lightning miss a three-pointer and Blake grabs the rebound gets the ball back to me. I head down the court again and see another shooting opportunity. I hesitate, pump fake, and WHACK. The defender hits my arm and gets the whistle. I'm up to the line for two.

Every player has a ritual before shooting free throws. I always dribble twice and picture the oil-stained spot next to the crack on my driveway where I practice.

DRIBBLE, DRIBBLE, BOING!

No way! It bounces off the rim!

DRIBBLE, DRIBBLE, SWISH!

It's good!

Finally! I put up a point, although I still haven't scored a field goal. I can hear my family cheering in the bleachers and Adam whistling. As I run back on defense, I can't help but think about all the mango milkshakes, rides to practices and games, one-on-one on the driveway, 2K battles, building my new basketball hoop, and trips to the doctor. It's like I can feel Nana Abu, Coach, Adam, Mama, Baba, Jamal Mamoo, Zara, my teammates, and friends carrying me, pushing me further, echoing my great grandfather's advice:

"Focus on what you *can* do, Zayd."

My shot may be off, but I can keep trying while I concentrate on defense, passing, and everything else I can do for now. We're still down 22–19 and only have six minutes left to play.

Over the next several minutes I turn it on and do my best impression of a determined

John Wall who's down in the fourth quarter. I hustle and have a couple of impressive passes and a few nice assists. I finally break the shooting slump and make a quick layup, a shot from inside the three-point line, and a pull-up jumper.

With a minute left in the game, I have seven points, three assists, a steal, and a rebound. It's much better than my first-half performance, but it's not enough to give us the lead. At least I know that no matter what happens, I've given it my all and done everything I can do.

The seconds are ticking by and we're down 28–27. It's our possession, and I pass the ball to Sam. He gets it knocked out of his hand by a defender. My heart sinks as I imagine the Lightning going on a fast break. Then Sam dives for the ball and manages to get it back! He tosses it to me, and I find Ravindu open. Ravindu drains the open shot.

"WOO-HOO!" I hear Zara scream.

And now I can't believe it—we're up by one! But it's the Lightning's ball, and they just need to score to win it all. Our entire season comes down to this play.

With twelve seconds left, the Lightning point guard looks confident as we cover them tight in man-to-man defense. It's as if we are gnats he can ignore. He passes it to number ten, who makes a move and blows by Sam.

But I'm quicker than number ten. Any thought of my ankle is history as I sprint down the court. I chase him down from behind. Then, right as he goes up for the layup, SMACK!

My block sends the ball soaring into the bleachers!

As the buzzer sounds, I'm smothered by my teammates in a gigantic group hug. I think we're jumping up and down in circles, or maybe it's the room spinning because it's hard to breathe. Either way, it's awesome.

I hear my family and Adam yelling and, when I look up, I see Adam standing and clapping. Naano and Nana Abu are beaming. Zara is doing a goofy dance. Baba is hugging himself. Mama is holding out her phone, and a tiny Jamal Mamoo is on the screen, hollering something I can't hear. I'm guessing he's yelling "Way to go, Skeletor!" I can't wait to tell him about my block and re-create it for him when he gets back. I'm going to relive this moment as often as I can.

Coach Wheeler comes around and gives

me a huge pat on the back that almost sends me flying forward.

"Incredible hustle out there, Zayd. That was some block," he says.

I'm already fired up and feeling confident, so I take a deep breath and decide to take a chance and ask for another thing I've been waiting for.

"So, Coach, do you think I could maybe be team captain next season?"

Coach frowns. He looks me up and down, like he's sizing me up. He scratches his head, and then starts to shake it slowly. I'm about to melt into the floor when he looks up at me and winks.

"Absolutely. You got it." He punches me lightly in the shoulder.

YES! I'm so overwhelmed and happy I can barely get the words out as I thank him.

I'm going to be captain of the gold team! The championship-winning gold team!

Then, just when I think the moment can't get any better, I hear my team chanting "MVP! MVP! MVP!"

And they're talking about me.